Please return / renew by date shown. DERCH
You can renew it at:
norlink.norfolk.gov.uk
or by telephone: 034
Please have your lib

D0489401

best to read ti.   ∪rder:

7. **Pig** and the Ice-cream Cake

8. **Pig** Skives off School

9. **Pig** is a Blue Baboon's Bottom

10. Super**Pig**!

11. **Pig** and the Baldy Cat

12. **Pig** Leaves Home (for a bit)

13. **Pig** tells a Whopping Great Fib

14. **Pig** is Hairy Snotter

15. **Pig** and the Rainbow Hair

16. **Pig** and the Big Quiz

17. **Pig** gets Angry

18. **Pig**'s Season's Finale   ... and more!

PIG and the Rainbow Hair
by Barbara Catchpole
Illustrated by Dynamo

Published by Ransom Publishing Ltd.
Unit 7, Brocklands Farm, West Meon, Hampshire
GU32 1JN, UK
www.ransom.co.uk

ISBN   978 178127 537 5
First published in 2015

and the
Rainbow
Hair

Barbara Catchpole

Illustrated by Dynamo

Ransom

Yellow

'Carrot head!'

'Baked bean bonce!'

'Ginger whinger!'

Dean Gosnall was shouting at me. He was spitting a bit too. I don't think he meant to be. It's just that his front teeth are huge.

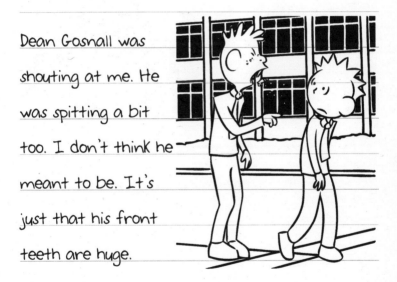

Actually, he looks like a huge hamster, or maybe

a rabbit, because he's got big ears, too.

He looks more like a
hamster than Harry
does. Dean Gosnall could
be in a horror film.
Probably 'Revenge of
the Killer Hamsters'.
We call him 'Goofy'.
Goofy Gosnall.

He was angry at me and shouting at me in
front of my friends. I felt horrible.

   'Wanna fight?'

No I didn't! My dad was in a fight once, down the pub.

My mum locked him out and he had to sleep round Gran's and then go to the dentist's and say sorry to the lady next door because he woke her up on a school night.

I didn't want to fight because:

1.   I had promised Mum I wouldn't fight – EVER – because she said it was for losers.

My dad always said:

    'He should stick up for himself, Siouxie!'

and my mum said:

    'Not with his fists, Wayne. Not if he wants

    to live in this house!'

2.   The teachers always got mad when

       there was a fight, and they were mad

       at me quite a lot anyway.

I didn't need to make them even
madder at me on purpose!

3.   I would get hurt. I am skinny and
     short. Dean was big and chunky. Do the
     maths. I'm not that daft!

I walked backwards a bit, away from Dean. Raj
and Tiff were suddenly standing at my side.

Were they going to help me fight Goofy Gosnall?
Raj, me and Tiff: The Three Musketeers
(whatever THEY are!).

Raj took his glasses off. I don't know why – he
can't see a thing without them. He might hit
me or Tiff instead of Dean!

Everything is a white fog to Raj if he takes his

glasses off. He always gets picked last for football because he can't see the goal. To be honest, he can't see the ball either. He once spent ten minutes looking for his shorts and then tried to put his legs through his shirt sleeves.

Anyway! Tiff was awesome. She did karate shapes with her hands and made a ninja noise:

'Wah! Wah!'

and yelled:

'I am a black belt in su-shi!'

Dean backed off. He wasn't scared of us, but he does fancy Tiff. He wasn't going to fight Tiff.

At the moment I think she's going out with Gary, but she used to go out with Dean (in between me and Sky and Sky's brother, Brook).

Dean got right up close to me. He had a zit on his nose, so I tried not to look at him. He said:

'You're gonna get it, Pig!'

He sprayed me with spit again, then ran off.

Raj turned to Tiff. He said:

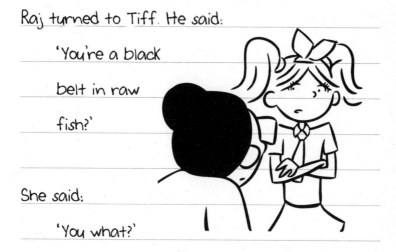

'You're a black
belt in raw
fish?'

She said:

'You what?'

Gran and Suki help me

So I went home.

Gran, Suki and Vampire Baby were all in the
kitchen. Gran was changing Vampire Baby's
nappy and talking to him.

'Ooose a sweet lil' diddums den?'

No wonder he's not talking yet. His first

sentence is going to be:

'I'm a lil' diddums!'

Suki was juggling fruit. She's getting nowhere

fast with her modelling career, so she's decided

to go on 'Britain's Got Talent' (on TV) juggling

unusual things.

She started by juggling with Vampire Baby, but Mum stopped that (although he thought it was great).

Then Suki tried juggling saucepans, but she knocked herself out and had to go to casualty. It took five hours to get seen and Mum missed 'Eastenders'.

Now Suki's destroying all our fruit. (That's OK with me. Fruit's a bit ... well, you know ...)

'What's up, bro?' Suki asked, as I walked in and

an apple hit me in the eye. I wasn't crying but it was raining a bit outside.

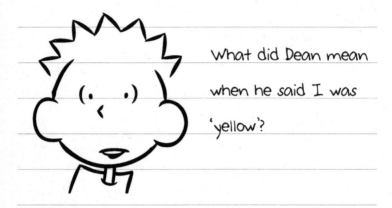

What did Dean mean when he said I was 'yellow'?

I asked Gran, because she'd probably know.

She says loads of weird stuff, like:

'He's like a duck with a broom.'

(Watching me making tea.)

'You're a long time dead.'

(Sadly whenever she wants a sixth biscuit.)

And my favourite:

'You're barking up the wrong tree.'

(When my mum says anything about

anything at all.)

If you ask Gran how old she is, instead of

saying 'seventy two and a half' she says:

'As old as my tongue and a little older than

my teeth,'

which is a lie

because she got her

teeth from the

dentist last month.

So Gran told me

what 'yellow' means.

'It means you're a coward, Pig! A scaredy-cat! A namby-pamby! A mummy's boy!'

'OK, Gran – I get it!'

Suki said:

'You ARE a wuss, Pig.'

Gran and Suki and I all have red hair.

So I thought I would get them on my side.
I should've kept my mouth shut. I should have
known what would happen. Gran is as bad as
Suki – out of control. But I didn't keep my
mouth shut. I said:

'It's because I've got red hair.'

Blue

Their mouths fell open. Then Suki said:

'Duh! I can fix that!'

and she rushed
upstairs and came
back with a box of
hair dye.

I asked:

'Isn't it dangerous? All them chemicals?'

Suki said:

'No.'

Then she said:

'It would be if you did it, 'cos you're only a kid. But Gran and me, we're like adults!'

I should have known. They're not that much like adults - more like giant six-year-olds!

Suki opened all the packets and little bottles of hair dye and mixed them all up. She and Gran started singing 'Dancing Queen' and messing around, scooping up all the purple bubbles and throwing them at each other.

Six-year-olds, see? Gran got loads of Mum's best white towels. In no time the kitchen was covered in mauve bubbles.

The bubbles got onto Vampire Baby and a big

part of his face was purple. Gran got it off
with a wipe. Then the bubbles fell onto Harry
and he went and sat in his toilet. They were
everywhere – great clouds of purple bubbles. Suki
rubbed the purple stuff into my hair and the
red disappeared.

I said:

'I don't want purple hair.'

Suki said:

'No, that's not the akchu-al colour. Purple's

not the akchu-al colour at all!'

They looked at each other in silence. Then they

looked at my head again.

Suki rinsed all the bubbles off. They both looked

at my head (again!). Suki grabbed the baby and

Gran grabbed her walking frame. They gave me

one last long look.

Then they burst out laughing. Suki held her
tummy as if her insides were going to explode.

Then she ran out the back door. Gran stomped
after her and I could hear them shrieking all
the way down the back alley.

I pulled out a couple of hairs and looked at
them. They were was bright blue! I had blue
hair!

Then I heard Mum's key in the lock. What was I going to do? She would kill me!

Green

I was sat next to Mum's best towels (they were blue), at the kitchen table (blue patches) next to Harry's cage. (Harry was bright blue. It suited him.)

Mum's mouth fell open and then closed. Then it fell open again. She looked like a goldfish.

Her face went red and then, all of a sudden, she started shouting.

'What has bloomin' Suki done? What the blue bonkers bloomin' blazes has she done

to your hair? That school won't let you in

with blue hair!'

No school! I thought that was a good thing,

anyway.

Then she said:

'Perhaps it'll wash out. That hamster will

have to stay blue though. Perhaps we can sell his picture to the paper.'

Harry doesn't like being washed – we tried it once and Dad needed stitches.

Mum got to work. She washed my hair. Still blue.

She washed it again in a tiny bit of washing-up liquid. Still blue.

She went a bit mad and mixed up loads of stuff from the kitchen cupboard: vinegar and lemon juice and marmite and cooking oil. She put it on my hair and left it for five minutes. It worked!

In a way, anyway.
The blue had gone,
but my hair had
turned green. And
I smelled like a bag
of chips.

Con Hair

Mum went spare!

'That Suki ... stroppy little madam ... no
more brains than that hamster ... just
wait 'til I get my hands on her ... mad as
two balloons ... just like her father ... can
move out and get her own place ... super
model – more like super moron ... just wait
'til she's got a family of her own!'

Then she ran out of puff and sat down and looked at me for a bit.

Finally she phoned her friend Connie who runs the Con Hair Salon in Cuttings Road. It was nearly closing time, so we got a taxi.

When we got there Connie was having a ciggie outside the shop.

'Blimey, Siouxsie, do you want me to cut his hair or mow it?'

(Ha ha. Green, you see. 'Mow it'. Ha ha. Not funny.)

'Just make it ginger again.'

Connie said she would do her best – and she did, because when she finished my hair was bright  orange. I mean BRIGHT orange – like an orange orange in the sunset in an orange fruit bowl in Orange Town.

It was dark as we walked home, but my hair lit up the road. Moths kept banging into my head.

Mum said:

'Why did you do it, Pig?'

I told her.

'I was being bullied. Dean was bullying me for no reason at all.'

'Hmm,' said Mum. 'Hmm ... '

When we got in, Mum sent me straight to bed with a slice of toast. No chips ever again, she said – we had spent all our chip money (forever!) on the cab fare!

She didn't stop there, either. She kept on going. If I was stupid enough to let Suki dye my hair,

she said, I didn't deserve chips. She didn't know what she had done to deserve such a daft son. God knows, she had tried. It was a wonder to her I could manage to breathe by myself. Why couldn't she have a son like Raj?

I stopped listening.

All evening I could hear her talking on the phone – every now and again her big laugh rang out. She was talking to a lot of people!

I thought I heard her
talk to Mrs Gosnall –
was she going to sort
her out? Mum is quite
a big lady, but Mrs
Gosnall is huge. She has
her own post code. She
has her own weather.

Red Hair Day

When I woke up the next morning, I didn't

want to go to school. I felt sick.

I was really worried because of my orange hair.

Dean was mean enough yesterday. What was he

going to say, now I looked like a satsuma on a

stick? He was going to start a fight. No doubt about it.

I was really scared. Don't tell anyone, will you?

Mum and I shouted at each other through the door. In my new bedroom she can shout at me in my bed without coming out of the kitchen. At least until Mrs Zielinski next door bangs on the wall, anyway.

'Get up, Pig!'

'I'm sick!'

'Get up, Pig!'

'I've got measles!'

'Now!'

'My head hurts!'

'Get ... '

'I'm all hot! I've got Hamster 'flu. They have to send men in white suits and keep me in a bubble in hospital and stuff. It's very sad!'

'Up!'

'Please Mum!'

'If you don't get up right now, I'm coming in there and I'll sling a bowl of cereal all over you and you'll still have to get up because you're nothing but trouble and I don't know why I bother with you! So if you don't want to go to school wearing your breakfast, get in here now, Peter Ian Green!'

I sat next to Harry, the World's Only Blue Hamster, and ate my breakfast. Then Mum marched me to school.

Oh no! She was coming in! I hate it when Mum comes into school. I like to keep her out. There's no need for Mum to know what I do in school and no need

for teachers to know my mum. They gang up on you.

I tried to get away, but Mum got hold of my coat and dragged me into assembly. Everyone was already in there. Perhaps we were late?

I stared at the floor, but when I looked up I couldn't believe what I was seeing. Everyone, but EVERYONE, had red hair!

The teachers all had red tinsel wigs – all except that attendance bloke who's got bright red hair anyway.

Miss Joseph, the head teacher, had a big curly

clown's wig. (The wig was curly – not the clown!
Got to be clear about these things!)

All my friends had clip-on red hair or spray can
streaks. Even Raj had a bright red cloth on his
long Sikh hair. A big banner above the stage
said 'Red Hair Day'.

Red assembly

The story in assembly was about red-haired people.

Eric the Viking had red hair (well duh!). His dad killed people and Eric also killed people and he got slung out of Iceland. He didn't sound like a very nice man.

Henry VIII also had red hair and used to chop off his wives' heads when he got fed up with them. (That's when he got fed up with his wives, not with just their heads. That would have been weird.)

Miss Joseph said:

'He chopped and changed,'

and we all laughed
and laughed – but
nobody got it.

Henry VIII
wasn't a very nice
man either and he
couldn't make his
mind up.

Winston Churchill who won World War II for
England had red hair as well (before he went
bald. Then I suppose he had red not-hair).

There's always a message in assembly. You think
it's just random stuff that the teachers sling

together the night before, but they always
manage to have a message.

I know, because nobody at our school ever
knows what the message is — so we see who can
say the silliest things.

Miss Joseph will say:

    'What's the message of this assembly,

    children?'

and loads of people will put up their hands and
say:

    'Aliens are going to take over the school!'

    'Don't put things up your nose!'

'Cheese is bad!'

which is silly
because the
message is nearly
always about
litter. We're just
winding her up.

I think the message for this assembly was:
people with red hair are tough (but not all that
nice).

Then Miss Joseph got all serious. She looked
weird being serious in a red clown wig. Then
Mrs Gosnall came into the hall! She went up the

steps to the stage. You could see it shaking a bit.

My mum went and stood the other side of Miss

Joseph.

RED HAIR DAY

You could hardly see Miss Joseph. She looked like

the ham in a ham roll.

Dean and I had to go and stand on the stage

too. I hate being up on the stage. It makes me want to fart. I held it in this time, though. Just as well – I sort of knew I was in trouble.

Also I was a bit worried the stage would collapse under the weight. I wanted to get off quickly!

Miss Joseph smiled at me. I was a bit scared. She doesn't often smile at me, and when she does I'm usually in trouble. She laughed when she found me in her secret toilet!

She said:

'I really care for the members of my
school. I like every one of you.'

(That's not what she said when I farted in the
Mayor's assembly. She said I was a disgrace
and had let everyone down.)

'We are all different, and that is a good
thing. Different is good! But sometimes a

boy or girl will bully another boy or girl because they are different. Dean was bullying Pig because Pig has red hair. Say 'sorry', Dean!'

Dean said 'Sorr-eee,' and then had to say it again properly, and then had to say it again loud enough for everyone to hear.

Then everyone clapped. That startled one of the little ones and there was a bit of a wait while his teacher took him out because he needed a wee (the kid not the teacher. Got to be clear about these things!). I don't think the kid made it because they didn't come back.

Then my mum said:

'And Pig was very rude to Dean as well, and he will say 'sorry'.'

I knew it! I knew it would be my fault in the end!

So I said 'sorry' in front of the whole assembly and Dean grinned. We had to shake hands. Everyone clapped and cheered. One of the little ones started to cry. Then the mums left the stage and I could feel it going up and down as they walked.

We had an awesome Red Hair Day. We learned all about hair and hairy heroes with red hair and we had red stuff for dinner. I've never had carrots together with baked beans before.

The red-haired dinner lady isn't supposed to give me baked beans, because they don't help my wind 'problem'. But she gave me loads.

And do you know what? I do feel differently about Dean Gosnall now.

I hate him more than ever. And his goofy teeth.

The next **PIG** book is

PIG
and the
Big Quiz

About the author

Barbara Catchpole was a teacher for thirty years and enjoyed every minute. She has three sons of her own who were always perfectly behaved and never gave her a second of worry.

Barbara also tells lies.